For Jess, John and Ollie
~C.L.

For Glen P.
~T.W.

First published in 1997 by Magi Publications
22 Manchester Street, London W1M 5PG

This edition published 1997

Text © 1997 Christine Leeson
Illustrations © 1997 Tim Warnes

Printed and bound in Belgium by Proost NV, Turnhout

ISBN 1 85430 409 7

DAVY'S SCARY JOURNEY

by Christine Leeson

illustrated by Tim Warnes

Davy Duckling lived with his mother
by a stream that flowed through a wood.

All summer long Davy paddled happily
in the water, but sometimes he watched
other birds flying high overhead,
and wondered what lay beyond the trees.

As summer ended, Davy watched the
swallows gathering on the branches of
the trees. They seemed to be whispering
and planning among themselves.
"What are you doing up there?" he called.

"We're getting ready to fly away
to warmer lands," said the swallows.
"Winter is too cold for us here."
Davy sighed. He wished he could
see new places, too.

"Can I come with you?" asked Davy.

"You?" laughed the oldest swallow.

"You could never keep up with us.

Our journey is too long and it's far too dangerous. We must cross wide green seas where sharks swim."

"We must swoop with the eagles over shining mountain peaks," said another.

"We must cross fiery deserts of burning sand, before we reach the grassy plains," said a third.

"And the plains are no place for a little duckling. You might get stepped on by a giraffe or eaten by a lion."

Davy stuck his beak in the air. "All right then, if you won't take me, I'll get there by myself – you'll see!" he quacked.

The very next day, Davy began his journey,
paddling downstream towards the sea.
Soon the stream left the trees and opened
out into a misty stretch of rippling water.
Davy could not see the other side.
"This must be the sea," he decided.
"I hope there are no sharks here."

The sea was very wide, and although the waves were not high, Davy had to paddle for an awfully long time. It seemed that it would take him for ever, but at long last he saw land, appearing mistily ahead of him in the distance.

Davy rested for a while before setting out again, and it was sunset by the time he reached the foot of the mountains.
"They are bigger than I thought," he said as he began his climb. He could barely scramble over the huge rocks.

Night was falling as he reached the mountain top.
"Now all I have to do is to get down again," thought Davy. "I hope I don't meet one of those eagles on the way."

Davy's climb down did not take long
as he slipped, slid and bounced his way
to the bottom. In front of him,
beyond a tangle of grass, stretched a
big desert! Strange shapes crouched
in the darkness, as Davy waddled out
across the gravel and sand.

"This desert doesn't feel very
fiery to me," thought Davy,
"but those wild animals
look scary. I just hope
they don't pounce!"

Davy trudged on through the night.
As the first gleam of sunrise lit the sky, he hauled
himself to the top of a low hill and saw the grassy
plains stretching far ahead.
"I'm here! I've made it!" shouted Davy, flapping
his stubby little wings in excitement as he ran
down the hill and on to the plain.

Suddenly, Davy stopped and looked up.
Many pairs of very long legs towered
above him.
"What strange animals!" he gasped.
"They must be those giraffes the swallows
were talking about."
Davy scuttled back to the safety of a bush.
He wanted to settle down for a nice nap . . .

. . . but another animal was waiting
for him in the shadows –
a tawny-coloured, yellow-eyed,
sharp-fanged one!

"A lion!" squeaked Davy, backing
away in fright.
The lion crouched, tensed itself
and leapt out of the bushes,
right on top of . . .

. . . Mother Duck!
"QUACK–QUACK–QUACK!" squawked
Mother Duck, pecking hard as she fought
off the fierce, spitting lion.

The lion bristled
and fled with
Mother Duck
flapping after it.
"Well, that's seen *him* off!" said Mother
Duck as she came back. "It looks as if I arrived
just in time. I've been searching for you all night,
you naughty duckling." She ruffled Davy's feathers.
"And now I think it's high time you came straight
home with me."
Davy agreed.
He had seen quite
enough of the world
for one day.

Davy hopped on to his mother's back
and they flew high into the air.

"Oh look, Mum!"
cried Davy. "You can
see everything from
up here!"
And so they could –
the grassy plains,
the fiery desert,
the mountains and the sea.
"Didn't I go a long way?" said Davy proudly.
"Why the swallows haven't even arrived yet!"